MS WIZ

Terence Blacker has been a full-time 1983. In addition to the best-selling *Ms Wiz* stories, he has written a number of books for children, including the *Hotshots* series, *The Great Denture Adventure, The Transfer, The Angel Factory* and *Homebird*.

What the reviewers have said about Ms Wiz:

"Every time I pick up a Ms Wiz, I'm totally spellbound . . . a wonderfully funny and exciting read." *Books for Keeps*

"Hilarious and hysterical." Susan Hill, *Sunday Times*

"Terence Blacker has created a splendid character in the magical Ms Wiz. Enormous fun." *The Scotsman*

"Sparkling zany humour . . . brilliantly funny." *Children's Books of the Year*

Titles in the Ms Wiz series

1. Ms Wiz Spells Trouble
2. In Stitches with Ms Wiz
3. You're Nicked, Ms Wiz
4. In Control, Ms Wiz?
5. Ms Wiz Goes Live
6. Ms Wiz – Banned!
7. Time Flies for Ms Wiz
8. Power-Crazy Ms Wiz
9. Ms Wiz Loves Dracula
10. You're Kidding, Ms Wiz
11. Ms Wiz, Supermodel
12. Ms Wiz Smells a Rat
13. Ms Wiz and the Sister of Doom
14. Ms Wiz Goes to Hollywood
15. Ms Wiz – Millionaire

Terence Blacker

Ms Wiz Goes Live

Illustrated by Tony Ross

MACMILLAN
CHILDREN'S BOOKS

First published 1990 by Piccadilly Press Ltd
Young Piper edition published 1991 by Pan Books

This edition published 1996 by Macmillan Children's Books
This edition produced 2001 for The Book People Ltd,
Hall Wood Avenue, Haydock, St Helens WA11 9UL

ISBN 0 330 34869 8

7 9 8 6

A CIP catalogue record for this book is available from
the British Library.

Phototypeset by Intype London Ltd
Printed by Mackays of Chatham plc, Chatham, Kent

CHAPTER ONE

Parent Problems

It was an evening like any other at the Smith household.

Mr Smith was in the living room reading a newspaper and drinking a can of beer. Mrs Smith was shouting at him from the kitchen. Caroline, their eldest child, was trying to do her homework and wondering what it was about parents that made them argue all the time. And her three-year-old sister, known to everyone as Little Musha, was in front of the television, carefully working some chocolate cake into the carpet.

There was a crash of cutlery from the kitchen.

"I work all day!" Mrs Smith said loudly. "And have you done the

washing-up when I come home, or cooked the children's supper, or done the hoovering or made the beds? Have you heck!"

"Yak yak yak," said Mr Smith, taking a swig of beer. "I've been out looking for a job. I'm tired."

Caroline sighed and took the remains of the chocolate cake from her little sister, who started crying.

There was another crash of plates from the kitchen. "All I can say," muttered Mrs Smith, "is that you've changed. You're not the man I married."

"That's true," said Mr Smith. "I was happy then."

"Happy!" Mrs Smith gave an angry laugh. "You've always been a miserable useless, lazy—"

"Mum," said Caroline, who knew exactly when to interrupt her parents' rows. "I'm trying to do my homework and Musha keeps trying to turn the television on."

"It's my favourite programme," said Musha.

"What is?" asked Caroline.

Musha thought for a moment. "Whatever's on now," she said.

"*Please* tell her, Mum—"

"STOP FIGHTING!" Their mother stamped her foot. A plate fell to the ground and smashed. There was silence for a moment. Mrs Smith sighed. "Let her watch television, Caro," she said. "At least, we get some peace that way."

"What about my homework?"

Mr Smith wandered into the kitchen. "I'm going to the pub," he mumbled.

"The *pub*?" gasped Mrs Smith.

"Why don't you both go out?" said Caroline, quickly joining them.

"Great idea," said her mother

tearfully. "We could go and watch a terrible film and grumble about it afterwards or eat at a restaurant and realize we have nothing to say to one another, or just watch other people having fun in a pub."

Mr Smith put his arm around his wife's shoulders. "Come on, love," he said. "Let's have an evening out. We both need a break."

"And what about a babysitter?" asked Mrs Smith.

Just then the doorbell rang. Caroline opened the door.

"Good evening," said a young woman with a clipboard under her arm. "I'm doing a survey for—"

"Ms Wiz!" Caroline smiled. "What on earth are you doing here?"

"I'm doing a survey for—"

"Hey, Mum, Dad," Caroline shouted over her shoulder. "This is Ms Wiz, who did all the magic things

at school and visited Jack in hospital and found Lizzie's stolen cat and saved the library by bringing Peter Rabbit and Frankenstein to life."

"Not that witch woman?" said Mr Smith suspiciously.

"Paranormal Operative actually," said Ms Wiz. "It's not quite the same."

"Can Paranormal Operatives babysit?" asked Mrs Smith.

"Well," said Ms Wiz. "I'm really here to complete this survey."

"What's it about, Ms Wiz?" asked Caroline. "Something magic?"

Ms Wiz looked at the clipboard and took a deep breath. "I need to know how many windows people have in their houses, how big the windows are, if they're happy with their windows and, if not, how they would like them changed, whether their windows go up and down or open sideways or slide, if they're draughty when the wind blows, whether they're made of wood or metal, how often the window cleaner comes, how much he charges, how many windows *he* has at home, does he wash them with a sponge or a cloth or bits of newspaper and does he whistle while he works and—"

"Boring," said Little Musha.

"I suppose it is rather," said Ms Wiz. "All right. I'll babysit for you." She stepped into the house.

"Are you reliable?" asked Mrs Smith.

"Reliable?" Caroline laughed. "She was a teacher. You can't be more reliable than that, can you?"

"Mmm," said Mr Smith uncertainly. "Wasn't there something about her keeping a rat up her sleeve?"

"That was just a rumour," said Caroline, handing her father his coat

and holding the front door open for him. "You both go out and enjoy yourselves."

Mumbling, Mr and Mrs Smith made their way out of the house. As Ms Wiz, Caroline and Little Musha waved them goodbye, they were arguing as to how they should spend the evening.

"Phew!" said Ms Wiz, closing the front door. She pulled a rat out of her sleeve. "Can Herbert have a run now?"

"Survey, eh?" said Caroline with a smile. "You knew I needed help."

Ms Wiz shrugged. "I go where magic's needed," she said. "So what's the problem here?"

Caroline frowned. "I always seem to be sorting things out. Musha, Mummy, Daddy. I'm only nine but I never have any fun these days."

"We'll see about that," said Ms Wiz.

Herbert, the magic rat, was scurrying towards the kitchen when Little Musha picked him up rather roughly.

"Don't like rats," she said, nose to nose with Herbert.

Ms Wiz smiled. "Not even rats with miniature water-pistols in their right ears?"

"What?" said Little Musha.

At that moment a jet of water

squirted from Herbert's right ear, hitting Little Musha in the eye. "Ow!" she shouted, dropping the rat and starting to cry.

When Little Musha cried, the glasses in the kitchen rattled, the neighbours shut their windows and cats disappeared up trees in terror at the noise. It was like a police siren.

"This is Little Musha," Caroline

shouted to Ms Wiz. "She's—"

Caroline remembered a phrase that grown-ups liked to use when discussing her sister "—she's quite a character."

"Little Musha, eh?" said Ms Wiz. "Is that a nice Indian name?"

Little Musha stopped crying. "I'm called Musha," she said, treading on Ms Wiz's toe, "because I mush people."

"Her real name's Annie," Caroline explained. "But she's going through a mushing phase and likes to be called Little Musha."

"Well, she had better not mush me," said Ms Wiz firmly. "And what are we going to do tonight, Little Musha?"

"Television."

"Oh no," said Caroline. "We could do amazing things now that Ms Wiz is here. She can turn people into animals, make things disappear. She can fly."

Musha thought for a moment. "Television," she said.

"See?" said Caroline. "No fun."

"What's wrong with television?" asked Ms Wiz.

"But we always watch—"

Ms Wiz held up her hand and smiled. "Trust me," she said.

CHAPTER TWO

Jimmy goes Bananas

"You're getting *smaller*, Ms Wiz!"

Caroline and Ms Wiz were watching the What-a-Load-of-Show-Offs Show on television when Little Musha began to stare at Ms Wiz.

"It's true," she said. "You really are getting smaller, Ms Wiz."

"Yes," said Ms Wiz. "I'm thinking of going into television."

"Oh no," said Caroline, who now saw that her sister was right and that Ms Wiz was shrinking rapidly. "Don't go all small on us. You're meant to be babysitting."

Ms Wiz was now slightly smaller than Little Musha. "You can shrink too, if you like," she said.

"But then what happens?" asked Caroline.

"We enjoy some television, from inside the television set."

"Yeah!" said Little Musha. "Do it, Ms Wiz."

When Ms Wiz was around, the strangest things seemed normal. Within seconds, Caroline discovered that the furniture in her living room appeared to have grown to an enormous size. A fly on a wall nearby looked as big as a jumbo jet.

"Follow me," said Ms Wiz to Caroline and Little Musha. They all climbed on to a nearby matchstick.

"Hold tight," shouted Ms Wiz as the sound of a low hum filled the room. The matchstick hovered above the ground and then carried the three of them on to the television set.

"What about Herbert?" asked Caroline.

"It's all right," said Ms Wiz. "He's in my pocket – as tiny as we are."

"I hate Herbert," muttered Little Musha, remembering the water pistol. "I hope he disappears altogether."

"Now how exactly are we going to get into this set?" Ms Wiz was tapping the top of the television. "Here we are," she said, opening a small trapdoor. Some steps led into the dark inside.

Little Musha gasped. "Ms Wiz is going into the telly," she said. "What are we going to do now?"

Caroline remembered that she was meant to be the responsible one. "But we're not even allowed to touch the back of the television because it's so dangerous," she shouted down the steps. "I don't think Mum and Dad would like it if we got right inside."

"Don't worry," Ms Wiz's voice echoed in the darkness. "This is magic TV."

"Come on then," said Little Musha.

Caroline sighed, took her little sister's hand and stepped into the television set.

"Ready?" said Ms Wiz, when they reached the bottom of the steps. In front of them was a large door with a notice saying "STUDIO 5 – DO NOT

ENTER WHEN THE RED LIGHT IS ON". The red light above the door shone brightly.

"What's the light for?" asked Caroline.

"It means they're making a programme," said Ms Wiz. "It's probably the one we were watching. Let's go in and see."

She opened the door and all three of them were dazzled by bright lights.

"And now," a voice was saying, "the What-a-Load-of-Show-Offs Show welcomes our next contestant."

As her eyes grew accustomed to the studio lights, Caroline saw a man with a yellow jersey walking towards them.

"It's Jimmy," she whispered. "He's the star of What-a-Load-of-Show-Offs."

"Yes," said Ms Wiz. "And we're on his show."

"I want to go home," said Little Musha.

Jimmy took her hand and held it tightly. "Hello, little girl," he said, putting his face close to Little Musha's. "And what's our name then?"

"Musha."

"Musha." Jimmy winked at the camera which had followed him across the studio. "What a lovely name. Why do they call you that?"

"Careful," Caroline murmured, but it was too late.

"Because I like mushing." Little Musha reached out for Jimmy's nose and twisted it hard.

"Aaaaagghh!" The star of What-a-Load-of-Show-Offs hopped from one foot to the other until Little Musha let go of his nose. "Aaaaggghhh . . . ha . . . ha . . . ha . . . Isn't live television great, folks?"

"Why have you got tears in your eyes?" asked Little Musha.

"I'll tell you after the show," said Jimmy through clenched teeth. "Come over here and play our lovely quiz game."

Ms Wiz and Caroline took a seat at the back of the studio as Little Musha reluctantly allowed herself to be led to a big chair.

"Now every time I say a word,"

said Jimmy. "You have to say another word that's a bit like it. So I say 'rain' and you say 'cloud' or 'sun' or 'wet'. All right?"

Little Musha nodded. Her chin was set like a boxer's before a fight. This was never a good sign.

Jimmy smiled. "Now—"

"Then," said Little Musha.

"I haven't started yet, *silly*."

"Billy," said Little Musha.

"No—"

"Yes."

"Very funny," said Jimmy, whose face was now a bright red colour. "The first word is . . . hair."

"Pull."

"Ice cream."

"Carpet."

"Bedtime."

"Scream."

"Toe."

"Stamp."

"Stamp?" said Jimmy. "That's not right, is it? Now where's the connection between toe and—"

Little Musha brought her sharp little heel down hard on Jimmy's toe.

"EEEERRRRGGGGHHHH!" Jimmy staggered back. "Where's a doctor? Where's my agent? Get this child out of here! I never wanted to work with children anyway. I was going to be an actor."

"I think we've outstayed our welcome," said Ms Wiz quietly to Caroline. "Get your sister and follow me."

"Someone take this little brute away," Jimmy was shouting.

Caroline hurried forward and grabbed Musha.

"That was fun," said Little Musha.

"Maybe for you," said Caroline, dragging her out of the studio. "For me, it's home from home. Now come *on*."

Ms Wiz was waiting for them at a door marked "EXIT".

"Don't like Jimmy," said Little Musha as they hurried out of the studio.

Ms Wiz sighed. "I don't think he's wild about you either," she said.

CHAPTER THREE

"No autographs, perlease!"

"No, of course you're not a little brute," said Caroline, holding Musha's hand as they hurried along a brightly-lit corridor. "Is she, Ms Wiz?"

"Certainly not," said Ms Wiz.

"Where are we going to now?" asked Little Musha.

"Let's try and find a programme with a bit less violence," said Ms Wiz. "If we go on like this, we could get banned from the television."

Caroline had an idea. "Maybe I could—"

"Hey," shouted Little Musha as they turned a corner. "Cartoons!"

"Oh, forget it," sighed Caroline.

Ahead of them, standing outside a

studio door, sipping tea, were two cartoon characters, a cat and a mouse.

Little Musha gasped. "It's Tom and Jerry," she said.

Jerry, the cartoon mouse, gave a weary smile. "No autographs, perlease," he said. "Not when we're resting between takes."

"I thought that Tom and you were meant to be enemies," said Caroline. "On television, you're always chasing each other about and hitting one another over the head."

"Don't believe everything you see on the screen," said Jerry. "We're enemies when the cameras roll but in real life, we're buddies."

"Real life!" Caroline smiled. "But you're cartoon characters."

"Hey, lady," said Jerry, putting on his well-known frown. "Don't knock cartoons, perlease. Like this evening, we're rehearsing a scene where Tom's

playing golf. He rolls me up into a little ball and wallops me three hundred yards. I bounce off a tree, rebound off a passing seagull, catch Tom in the stomach and flatten him against a wall, which then collapses on top of him."

"You *rehearse* that?" asked Caroline.

"How else d'you think we get it right?" said Tom. "Magic?"

"The producer says we could use stand-ins but we like to do our own stunts," said Jerry. "Talking of which, it's time for me to run Tom over with a steamroller."

Tom winked. "Showbiz!" he said. "Don't you just love it?"

"Can I come?" asked Little Musha.

"No," said Ms Wiz and Caroline at the same time. Musha took a deep breath, sniffed a couple of times and burst into tears at maximum volume.

A woman hurried down the corridor towards them.

"*Ssshhh!*" she went. "How can we make television programmes with that terrible din? We've already had a disaster tonight with Jimmy throwing a tantrum on the What-a-Load-of-Show-Offs Show."

"Oh dear," said Ms Wiz, trying to keep a straight face. "We wouldn't know about that. We're just here on a visit."

"And what exactly are you here to see?" asked the woman.

Caroline put up a hand. "I was hoping—"

"We're looking for a really nice show," Ms Wiz interrupted.

"Nice?" The woman scratched her head. "There's not much demand for that these days. I suppose you could try our new series, Wild, Woolly and Weally Intewesting. They're doing a programme on extinct species at the moment, downstairs in Studio 9B."

The red light outside Studio 9B was shining brightly and there was a sign on the door which said, "QUIET! EXTINCT ANIMALS – DO NOT DISTURB!"

"What does extinct mean?" asked Little Musha.

"It means that they're the type of animals that no longer exist in the world," said Caroline.

"How can they be disturbed then?"

"I think it's a sort of television joke," said Ms Wiz, gently pushing the studio door open.

"Wow!" said Caroline.

Studio 9B had been decorated like a jungle, full of trees and creepers and the sound of exotic birds. In the centre of the studio, a big man with a beard was talking breathlessly in front of a camera.

"And so," he said. "Over litewally hundweds of centuwies, species changed, evolved and adapted to the world's enviwonment. If they haven't changed, many of them have pewished, died out, become extinct. Like—" the man walked across the studio to where a model of a strange-looking animal stood "—like Tywannosauwus Wex."

"Why aren't the animals moving?" whispered Little Musha.

"Because they're extinct," said Caroline.

A faint humming noise was coming from Ms Wiz. "I wonder if this programme needs livening up," she said.

"And then," the bearded man continued, "there's the dodo, a bird that died out almost two hundwed years ago." He walked to where Ms

Wiz stood. "Here we have a stuffed model of the dodo – as you can see, it's vewy vewy dead and extinct."

At that moment, the dodo put its head on one side and pecked at something on the studio floor.

"Now that's weally wather stwange," said the bearded man nervously. "Extinct animals don't usually move like that."

The dodo flapped its wings and flew on to a branch. "*Vewy* odd,' said the television presenter, scratching his beard. "The dodo can't fly. Or couldn't fly. I think I must be dweaming."

"Off you go, Herbert," muttered Ms Wiz, releasing the magic rat from her sleeve. Herbert stood on her arm, then spread his front legs and started to fly, like a small bird. After circling around Ms Wiz a couple of times, he flew across the studio.

The bearded man was climbing the tree towards the dodo when he noticed Herbert, hovering delicately a few inches away from his nose.

"Good gwacious me!" he said with a hint of panic in his voice. "This looks vewy like a type of humming-bird, except it's a wat – it's a sort of humming-wat." He sat down heavily on a branch. "I must be ill. I'm seeing things," he said. "Turn the wuddy camewas off."

"Cut!" The loud shout came from a man in shirtsleeves who was now hurrying across the studio.

"What on earth's going on?" he asked.

"The dodo was alive," said the bearded man weakly. "Then I was buzzed by a humming-wat."

"The dodo?' The man in shirtsleeves looked up at the tree, where now the stuffed dodo was standing lifelessly. "Who put it up there?"

"It flew," moaned the bearded man. "And then I saw a humming-wat."

"Come on," said Ms Wiz, quietly putting Herbert up her sleeve. "I think it's time for us all to leave the jungle."

"So why don't you magic lots of extinct animals back to life?" Caroline asked after they had crept out of Studio 9B. "I'd love to see a real live dinosaur."

"My spells don't last that long," said Ms Wiz. "A few minutes at the mo—"

"Excuse me," said a woman, hurrying down the corridor towards them. "Are you the replacement newsreader?"

"Newsreader?" said Ms Wiz. "Ah, yes. That's me."

"Andrew, our normal reader, has a terrible cold and has completely lost his voice," said the woman. "You're on the air in five minutes so you had all better follow me."

"News?" said Caroline. "I thought we were here for fun."

"We are," said Ms Wiz. "I think this could be tremendous fun."

"But what about—?"

"Right," said Ms Wiz, turning to the woman. "Where's my studio?" she said.

CHAPTER FOUR

Good News for Really Nice People

"It's coming up to ten o'clock and, in a few seconds' time, we'll be going over to the newsroom for the news, read by Dolores Wisdom."

Caroline and Little Musha sat in a small room next door to where Ms Wiz was about to read the news and watched her through a big window between the two rooms. Beside them sat the producer, who was looking very nervous.

"She has done this before, hasn't she?" he asked Caroline.

"Probably," said Caroline.

"Because once she's started, we can't interrupt her, you know," warned the producer. "This is going out live."

"I'm sure she'll make it really . . . entertaining," said Caroline.

"Entertaining?" The producer looked more worried than ever. "I just want her to read the words on the little screen in front of her." He looked at a clock on the wall.

"Cue, Miss Wisdom," he said, holding his hand up.

"Good evening," said Ms Wiz, wearing her most serious expression

and reading the words in front of her. "It's ten o'clock and here are the news headlines. There has been a plane crash in Italy. The economy is looking worse than ever. The government says it's everyone else's fault. More wind and rain are forecast throughout the country. A famous actor has died. And—" Ms Wiz hesitated for a moment and said, "This is all a bit depressing, isn't it?"

"Hang on," said the producer next door. "Depressing? That wasn't in the script."

"You can hear all the gloomy news somewhere else," said Ms Wiz with a smile. "In the meantime, here's the good news for really nice people. Mr and Mrs Smith of 91 Elmtree Road went out tonight and had a very enjoyable time—"

"Whaaaaat?" said the producer. "Has she gone mad?"

"This," continued Ms Wiz, "after a grim start to the evening, during which Mrs Smith called Mr Smith miserable and lazy and then broke a plate—"

"How did she know that?" asked Little Musha.

"Listening at the door, probably," said Caroline.

"—but all has ended well, with the Smiths enjoying some fish and chips, just like the old days, followed by a romantic walk in the park. Their children, Caroline and Musha, have been shrunk by the babysitter."

The producer was now standing in front of the window and waving wildly at Ms Wiz, who waved back before going on with the news.

"Rats are getting nicer, it was officially announced tonight. And we have a rat spokesperson with us in the studio." Ms Wiz pulled Herbert the rat out of her sleeve. "So, Mr Herbert," she said. "Why have you rats suddenly decided to clean up your act?"

"Basically," said Herbert, looking towards the camera, "we're tired of the bad publicity. People say we're unfriendly, dirty and spread diseases and frankly, at the end of the day, this is not what we're about."

"And so what will you be doing about it?"

"First of all, we'll be cleaning our teeth," said Herbert. "There's no doubt that bright yellow teeth in a rat gives a very bad first impression. Then we'll be taking baths every day, and generally coming out of the closet and joining family life, rolling playfully around on the carpet, playing with the kids and so on."

"What about cats?" asked Ms Wiz.

"That's still a bit of a grey area," said Herbert. "But we hope to negotiate a peace settlement with them very soon."

"Thank you, Mr Herbert," said Ms Wiz, opening her sleeve so that he could return home. "That's really nice news."

"I've had enough," said the producer, getting to his feet. "I'm going to shut that woman up and read the news myself."

"And there's also good news for Paranormal Operatives," Ms Wiz was saying, when the producer walked briskly into the news studio. He was just about to lift Ms Wiz out of her chair when viewers throughout the country heard a faint humming noise. There was a flash of smoke – and there, in the place of the producer, stood a panda, blinking its eyes in the studio lights.

"We've just received a late news flash," said Ms Wiz. "A television producer has been turned into a panda. As everyone knows, the panda is a threatened species. In fact—" Ms Wiz pulled the panda's ear "—I'm threatening this one right now."

The panda slunk miserably out of the studio.

"Can I have a ride?" asked Little Musha, climbing on its broad back as it returned to the control room.

"As I was saying," Ms Wiz smiled at the camera, "the good news for Paranormal Operatives is that the word 'witch' is to be banned from dictionaries. I asked a well-known Paranormal Operative – me – why the ban was necessary. 'Well,' I answered myself, 'the word "witch"

suggests to a lot of people that to be magic you have to be an ugly old woman with cobwebs in your hair. This, of course, isn't true.' 'Why not?' I asked. 'Because,' I replied, 'magic belongs to all ages and to men as well as women, although, between me and me, women are rather better at it.' 'Thank you, Ms Wiz'," said Ms Wiz.

"This is getting very strange," said Caroline.

"Finally news of a really nice record achieved today. Little Musha Smith of 91 Elmtree Road has stayed up after ten o'clock and only burst into tears once. 'We're really proud of her,' said sister Caroline. 'Apart from pulling Jimmy's nose and then stamping on his foot, she has been an angel'."

"Hey, Musha," Caroline called out. "You're on the news."

But Little Musha was too busy riding the panda to pay any attention.

"Typical," sighed Caroline.

CHAPTER FIVE

A Lovely Perf

For a girl who had spent the evening inside her parents' television set with her favourite Paranormal Operative and a little sister who was now behaving quite well, Caroline was feeling surprisingly sad.

"Heigh-ho," Ms Wiz was saying, as they wandered along yet another corridor. "I really enjoyed that."

"You did seem to be having quite a lot of fun," said Caroline pointedly. "Just like Little Musha had quite a lot of fun earlier. Almost everyone has been having fun."

Ms Wiz smiled. "Anyway," she said, "we'd better head back to the real world. Your mum and dad will be home soon."

"I'm going to tell them about pulling Jimmy's nose," said Little Musha.

"What about my newsreading?" Ms Wiz laughed. "I always wanted to do that. The producer was quite upset about it."

"He'd still be galumphing about as a panda if I hadn't reminded you to turn him back into a producer," said Caroline quietly.

"Yes, thank goodness you were there," said Ms Wiz.

"I'm always there," said Caroline grumpily. "It's just like home in this television set. I keep Musha out of trouble. I even have to sort things out when the great Ms Wiz is having a good time. Why have I always got to be sensible and grown-up? When is it my turn to enjoy myself?"

Ms Wiz gave a little smile as they

walked past a door marked "GREEN ROOM".

"That's where the actors rest," she said. "Hey, you like acting, don't you, Caroline? Would you like to see if there's anyone there?"

Caroline shrugged. "If you like," she said.

Ms Wiz opened the door to reveal a man and a woman in Victorian costume. They both were pacing backwards and forwards and seemed rather upset.

"Wow," whispered Caroline. "It's Nigel Triffroll and Dulcima de Trop, the famous actors."

"What have I *always* said?" Nigel was clasping his brow. "Never agree to act with children or animals."

"And that ghastly little Jane was a bit of both," said Dulcima, fanning herself with a copy of *The Stage*.

"Very droll, darling," said Nigel.

"What appears to be the trouble?" asked Ms Wiz.

The two actors turned to them without showing the least surprise.

"Only that the little brute of a small girl who was supposed to appear in the last episode of Heritage, our wonderful costume drama, has got tonsillitis," said Dulcima.

"Tonsillitis, hah!" cried Nigel with a dismissive wave of the arm. "Otherwise known as stage fright."

"Why don't I do it?" asked Caroline.

Nigel and Dulcima looked at her in amazement.

"Are you a thesp?" asked Nigel.

"A what?"

Nigel sighed with impatience. "Do you tread the boards?" he said.

"If you mean, 'Does she act?'," said Ms Wiz. "The answer is, 'Yes, brilliantly'."

"Saved!" cried Dulcima. "Here are your lines." She gave Caroline a script. "Are you a quick learner?"

Caroline gulped. "Er, quite," she said nervously.

"The part you play is of a scruffy little chimney-sweep girl who turns out to be the Duchess of Portland," said Nigel. "Just be yourself, darling."

"We're on in five minutes," said Dulcima, grabbing Caroline's hand.

"I'll take you to make-up and we can learn the lines together."

"Why's Caroline all dirty?" asked Little Musha a few minutes later, as she and Ms Wiz watched Heritage on a small television in the Green Room.

"Ssshhh!" said Ms Wiz, sitting nervously on the edge of her seat. "I think she's the best chimney-sweep I've ever seen on television."

At that moment, the camera closed in dramatically upon Caroline's face. "You mean," she said, as tears welled up in her eyes. "You mean that I'm your *daughter*?"

"Welcome, home," said Dulcima with a dazzling smile.

As Nigel, Dulcima and Caroline embraced, the theme music for Heritage swelled up behind them.

"Did Caroline do well?" asked Little Musha.

"She was astonishing," said Ms Wiz, dabbing her eyes.

Moments later, the door to the Green Room was flung open and the three actors entered.

"A star is born!" announced Dulcima. "Caroline, you were wonderful, darling. Wasn't she wonderful, Nigel?"

"Lovely perf," said Nigel, adding with a hint of sulkiness, " I didn't think I was bad either."

"You were wonderful too," said Caroline.

Ms Wiz looked at a nearby clock. "Never mind the 'wonderful darlings'," she said. "If we don't hurry, your parents will be returning to an empty house."

"What about my clothes?" asked Caroline.

"Here they are," said Ms Wiz. "There's no time to take the soot off your face."

Caroline wriggled out of her clothes. "Bye, Nigel and Dulcie," she said breathlessly. "That was definitely the best fun I've ever had."

"Cheery-bye, darling," said Nigel.

Dulcima gave Caroline a kiss. "Will we be able to work together again soon?" she asked.

"I hope so," said Caroline.

Ms Wiz, Caroline and Little Musha ran as fast as they could down a long corridor.

"What about Herbert?" gasped Musha.

"I thought you didn't like rats," said Caroline.

"Poor Herbert! Left alone in television land."

"Don't worry," shouted Ms Wiz. "I've got him."

They ran up the stairs and through a trapdoor at the top.

"Home!" said Little Musha as, once again, they stood on top of the Smiths' television set. Just then, they all heard the sound of a key turning in the front door.

"Quick, Ms Wiz!" said Caroline. "Get us back to our normal size before my parents come in."

There was a humming noise from

the direction of Ms Wiz, and the next thing Caroline and Little Musha knew, they had fallen in a heap on the living-room floor. Everything in the room appeared to be back to normal.

"Well," said Mrs Smith, looking at the tangle of bodies on the floor. "Still up at eleven o'clock? I don't call that very good babysitting."

"We couldn't sleep," said Caroline. "I thought that, because tomorrow's

Saturday, it wouldn't matter too much."

"It doesn't," said Mr Smith, putting his arm around his wife's waist. "We've had a good time, so why shouldn't you?"

"Caroline," said Mrs Smith. "Your face is absolutely filthy. What have you been doing?"

Just then, the telephone rang. Mr and Mrs Smith looked at one another in surprise.

"Hullo," said Mrs Smith into the phone. "Yes . . . brilliant, I see. Could you call tomorrow after I've discussed it with her and her father?"

"Who was it?" asked Mr Smith.

"It was a television producer," said Mrs Smith, looking puzzled. "He told me he thought Caroline was so good in something called Heritage, he wanted her to act in other programmes."

"Perhaps you ought to tell them

about it, Ms Wiz," smiled Caroline.

"Ms Wiz!" gasped Little Musha. "You're getting *smaller*!"

"Oh no!" said Caroline. "Don't leave me to explain it all."

Ms Wiz winked. "Whenever magic's needed, I'll be back," she said, smiling at Caroline. "Magic – and fun."

"I can't believe my eyes," said Mr Smith.

"She's really tiny now," said Little Musha. There was a little pop, like a bubble bursting, and Ms Wiz had disappeared.

For a moment, the Smith family stood in silence.

"Could you kindly tell us what's been going on?" said Mrs Smith finally.

"It's a long story," said Caroline. "And I think you had better sit down first."